Praise for
Itzá:

"*Itzá* is full of magic, death, water, memories, beauty, and pain. This is a narrative about womanhood that's packed with blood and multiculturalism. This bilingual scream of resistencia is exactly what frontera fiction should be, and Rios de la Luz is a word bruja of the highest order."

— Gabino Iglesias, author of
Zero Saints and *Hungry Darkness*

"I love this book with my whole body. FINALLY a book, body and voice rising up from the edges of culture to say I am not dead, you cannot kill me, we are coming to take our stories back. Rios de la Luz is among the most important emerging writers of our time, or any time, because she is inventing a new language without limits that explodes all walls and borders meant to keep us small and quiet. Weaving fabula with domestic trauma and sexual becoming, Itzá restories a girl's life and identity up and through the violence of a culture that cannot contain her. Like a new species facing off with death heads. Like myth rupturing the lies we are told about who we are. Like an Xicana gender fluid voice and body ready to rearrange your reality, gloriously and without apology."

— Lidia Yuknavitch, author of
The Small Backs of Children and *The Book of Joan*

Praise for
The Pulse between Dimensions and the Desert:

"Another heart-wrenching first is *The Pulse between Dimensions and the Desert* by Rios de la Luz, a collection from Ladybox, the new imprint of Broken River Books. This collection of prose-poems and short fiction is a powerful exploration of Latina womanhood, shifting geographies, perspectives, languages and genre in a masterfully managed kaleidoscope. De la Luz often uses the trappings of speculative fiction (time travel, multiple dimensions, aliens) to approach subtle and complex human experiences in novel ways to devastating effect. Bursting with love, anger, hurt, hunger and unquenchable fire, *The Pulse between Dimensions and the Desert* will fling you beyond yourself and then kiss your shattered soul."

— David Bowles, *The Monitor*

"Rios de la Luz's writing blows minds and breaks hearts. A sort of new and bizarre Tomás Rivera, Rios is able to blend the familiar of the domestic with the all the wilderness of the universe. Her stories will grab you in places you didn't know you had, take you by those places to where you've always wanted to go— though you never knew how to get there. Buy this book and enjoy that journey."

— Brian Allen Carr, author of *Sip*

"In *The Pulse between Dimensions and the Desert*, Rios de la Luz's writing is electric and alive. It grabs you and pulls you into her universe, one that is both familiar and foreign, a place where Martians find love, bad guys get their ears cut off, and time travel agents save lost children. In this innovative, heartfelt debut, de la Luz takes her place as a young author that demands to be read and watched."

— Juliet Escoria, author of
Black Cloud and *Witch Hunt*

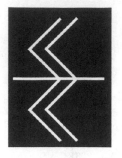

A Broken River Books original

Broken River Books
El Paso, TX

Interior design by J David Osborne

ISBN: 978-1-940885-41-4

Printed in the USA.

ITZÁ

by
Rios de la Luz

BROKEN RIVER BOOKS

EL PASO, TX

For Alma Rosa Rivera

and Meliza Bañales-Van

Table of Contents

Part 1

La Familia

Great-grandma: Abuelita Araceli

Grandma: Abuela Rubí

Mami: Magdalena

Oldest Sister: Marisol

Baby Sister: Araceli

PART 1

Itzá

Great-grandma, also known as Abuelita, died in her sleep. Her bed was in the middle of the forest. Yellow leaves sprinkled her bed. A giant maple leaf covered her face. Her long white hair spread above her head and reached the edges of the bed. Mushrooms bloomed out of the mattress. Mist permeated between the trunks of the forest trees as the branches looked down on Abuelita. We don't know how her bed got out there. We told the neighbors it was her dream to wander in the forest as a ghost. As a ghost, she can blend with the fog and follow rivers slithering into creeks. She can pick up after litter bugs and flick the backs of their heads. She can hiss into the ears of deer to ask them where the best berries are. She can follow hunters with their rifles, to see if ghosts have more power than guns.

We told the neighbors Abuelita loved climbing trees. When I think of her now, I see her up high on a tree branch eating mangoes or sardines. She loved messy foods and smelly foods. She loved crunching the bones of the tiny fish and then cackling about being a water witch. She loved wiping the nectar of fruit from her neck with the back of her hand. She taught me to devour plates of food with moans and laughter and sloppiness.

It took four days to drive to her. Mami drove along the coast and told us to take in the ocean. She told us to breathe in the mist and the salt of our own bodies. On our way to Abuelita's bed, the yellowing trees looked like enormous marigolds scattered along the rolling hills. We had marigolds in our laps, and candles lined the trunk of the car. Our faces painted into skulls, we sat still, held in our tears. We wanted Abuelita to witness us in our next bodies. Our decomposing future bodies. The ones sleeping in the earth. We wore white as we hiked through the forest. We wore white because of her hair. I whispered into the mist. I wanted to know if I was a water witch. Did Abuelita pass her bruja intuition down to me? Silence struck the forest. A strip of light pointed to a fragmented yellow leaf on the wet ground. I ran toward the leaf and held it to my chest. As I looked up, a heavy droplet of water fell onto the center of my forehead. I gasped and let the water trickle down my crooked nose.

Burial

Abuela's favorite color was lemon yellow because it made her brown skin illuminate. She compared her skin to the gleaming wings of dragonflies and the shimmering ruby throats of hummingbirds. *Mija, look at me glow. The sun kisses our skin, mija. Look at the veins in my arms and my hands, they pop out with electricity because I am so full of history and chisme.* In her lemon yellow pantsuit and deep brown beautiful skin, she went to church and sat in the front row so the priest could see how bright she dressed for her god. After church, Abuela sipped on café con leche and tongued her teeth. *Pos, los hombres discuss god in front of*

4

a crowd, but mujeres, we talk to god all day and we see god in everything, mija.

Even with a devout tongue, Abuela made her living day-to-day rules clear. Abuela forbade the entire family from wearing shades of yellow even into her death. For her funeral, we wore red. Red because it represented the blood pulsating inside of our vulnerable bodies. Red because her name was Rubí. Red to remind us she isn't fully gone. She passed down her precious stories and history into our blood. Now, she is an ancestor meant to hear us when we shout or whisper our prayers. *Pos, spread rumors about me if you want, just don't forget me, mija.*

Abuela lived with us during her final years. Her recliner was light purple and velvet comfort. I used to spell my name out on the sides of it while she watched her shows about haunted houses. After she passed, I could feel her presence in the empty living room when I walked by the recliner at night. I wanted to rock back and forth in her lap, but she was more than a ghost, she was veins of lightning, she was white swirling clouds, she was pollen sticking to the legs of honeybees. I never sat in her chair after her death, just in case she was resting there. I didn't want to make her uncomfortable. The recliner felt like a throne when I was a kid. Your butt melded into the cushion. It smelled like roses and Avon lotion. I was an astronaut in her purple chair, I counted down from three, two, one. Blast off. Then I farted into the cushion or burped out my lungs. Abuela used to peel me out of her recliner and laugh at my flatulence. *Pos, this is what our bodies do, mija. We expel smells and noises, it's just your body talking to you, mija.*

Skin

Araceli loved chewing the sides of skin next to the nail beds of her fingers. Sometimes, she saved the bits of skin in ashtrays. She told her older sister Marisol she planned on burning them in a ceremony. These were the pieces of herself she could send into the sky.

Araceli was petrified of death, so she tore apart pieces of herself to feel control and to feel animalistic. She wanted to feel closer to wolves and creatures who only bite out of fear and, at times, necessity. Araceli bit her nails off every full moon, out of superstition, so they grew stronger and faster after each renewal. She saved her nails in a tin bin previously occupied by stamps, thread, and prior to that, cookies. She buried the nails in the backyard while everyone inside the Mango House fell into their dreams. She dug a hole with no nails, inhaled the earth, and then gently placed the tin bin back under ground.

She prayed as she looked at the moon. She was thankful for parts of her that grew in likeness to plants. There were so many parts of her with roots. Her hair, her nails, her teeth, the nerves in her body reaching and filling the interior of her like the roots of redwood trees, unapologetic in the space they held onto because these were parts of her existence, parts she needed to survive and remain alive. She thanked the moon for the roots in her passed-down name. Araceli was named after her great-grandmother, the matriarch with brilliant white hair, what Araceli imagined heaven was like. She buried her nails and kissed the earth and then went to bed next to Marisol on their twin bed.

Araceli woke up to a bright light beaming through the bedroom window. In black and white, Araceli opened her mouth and light shot out of her face.

Her mouth, her eyes, her nose. Green roots sprouted from her fingers. Tiny green birds circled around her. Cawing and whistling. There was fear for a matter of seconds. Araceli's body stopped mutating as she turned around to see her abuelita. Araceli grabbed her great-grandmother's hands and kissed them. She missed her warmth. She missed her guidance. Abuelita held her and told her one myth and one truth about the future, but when Araceli woke up she couldn't remember what her namesake said.

Caminando con Abuela

Abuela tells me I don't have to believe everything she says to me. She confesses. She's lied to me on three occasions and she may never utter the truth. *Pos, no soy mentirosa, pero necesito mis propios secretos.* We walk past the barking armies of Chihuahuas and the women scrubbing and hanging their colorful clothes together. Doña Violeta is talking to her chickens and rabbits as we wave to her. She hands Abuela a white candle. Doña Violeta refuses to see her late husband, Otaniel. So, she gives Abuela a candle and a sealed letter and asks her to read it to him. Otaniel was unfaithful to her for many years of their marriage and only fessed up to his wandering eye when he was close to passing onto his next life. We walk past spilt confetti from the one-year birthday party last night. I pick some off the floor to give to Don Otaniel. I know Doña Violeta loved him and I don't know if one impulsive characteristic means someone is altogether rotten.

My purple backpack gently tap, tap, taps my lower back as I skip beside Abuela. We go to the cemetery on random days. Abuela explains it has to do with her dreaming patterns. I ask her to teach me how to remember my dreams. All I know is I fall into a deep black space and it's comfortable. I ask Abuela if she can teach me how to walk alongside her as she dreams. She promises to teach me when I get older.

Abuela knocks on the gate of the cemetery and a flock of crows spreads out into the blue sky. She opens the gate to see white petals cover the grass in between the graves. Candles sit atop of tombs and lipstick stains cover the photographs of a young man in a graduation gown. One gravestone is covered in lavender thread and small purple handprints. A letter rests under the thread. Some of the tombstones are built so high, you can see them from our house, about a mile away from the cemetery. Birds trade shifts on the tallest grave.

Abuela tells me building a final resting place as high as a skyscraper doesn't necessarily mean more adoration. It could be guilt, or regret. What do we do when we haven't said everything we mean to say and then the person is gone the next morning? *Pos, nada mija, no podemos hacer nada.* But we can build a skyscraper tomb and climb it when no one is around. We can scream at the sky or just pray. Closer to the clouds, we can admit all those things we are holding in for the dead.

From the gut

The only time Abuelita bit her tongue was in front of her great-grandchildren, Marisol and Araceli. They ran errands in the city on the weekends. Abuelita needed to visit the pharmacy. Marisol wanted to find her first tarot deck. Araceli wanted to watch the pigeons downtown to see if any of them were curious enough to follow her back home. As they waited at the bus stop for their ride home, a pale man with yellow hair stood in front of Abuelita, smirked, and called her a wetback. *Go back to where you came from. Drown on the way back.*

In an alternate reality, Abuelita's floral scarf covers Marisol and Araceli's ears. The world becomes mute to them. Lightning scratches at the sky to distract them from an ugly moment on the planet. Abuelita spits on the ground and sticks her fists through the man's chest. She asks him if the blood coming out of the orifice in his soul is just as brilliant red as the blood pumping into her vibrating heart. She slaps him across the face with her bloody hand and tells him to stop perpetuating the violence of his ancestors, stop being so simple and predictable, stop the infatuation with claiming bodies like hers unworthy of existing in the same space. She tells him in her gorgeous thick accent, *I have always been here and I will never leave. I don't owe you a god damn thing on this spinning earth because you are nothing, you are so small, so minute, I won't even keep a memory of your face, you white demon piece of shit.*

In this reality, Abuelita says nothing because she's recovering from the flu. The air is pushed out of her and she struggles to inhale. She is silent and looks past him. This is the silence that ejects you out of your body. It untangles every single hair on your skin and all of it stands up. You want to rip it out, you want to rip yourself into particles. It's so much more than a word or a phrase or a look. It is detaching yourself from your own body to step outside of it and ask why anyone would go out of their way to belittle you. It is white supremacy embedded into this social fabric, it is this reality that wants you gone, it is desperate to erase you. It's so much more and you cannot understand it unless it has happened to you. Unless, it keeps happening to you. You have to remind yourself about survival at all costs. You must survive at all costs.

Abuelita's hands shake as she grabs Marisol and Araceli by their small beautiful brown hands. The two girls stay quiet. Araceli breaks the silence. She exclaims to Abuelita, she knows for sure-for sure that they are a family of water witches. She keeps having dreams in aquamarine hues and she swears she was born to swim across oceans. Abuelita smiles and squeezes their hands. She begins to feel faint. She lets go of their hands and reaches for Marisol. She embraces Marisol's face and tells her she is enough. She caresses Araceli's face and tells her she is enough. *We deserve to exist.*

Drenched

Rain poured out of the dark clouds. Araceli held her arms out, opened her mouth, and stuck out her tongue. She called the sky the ultimate hydration station. She called out to Abuela, and in a matter of seconds, in bare feet and a lemon yellow tracksuit, Abuela came out to feel the water on her face. Marisol followed with her shaved head. Her head was an homage to Abuelita during the Year of Tenacious Hair. The water trickled off her round head and landed on the shoulder pads of her tangerine dress. Araceli was obsessed with any pigmentation of blue. She wore matching sky blue shorts and a shirt with patterned white clouds dispersed on the cotton. Her teal socks were drenched and squished in between her toes. She loved the weight of wet clothes, she loved feeling heavier than gravity meant to make her, she loved flailing herself around and stumbling over her own body. She loved feeling spastic. Araceli watched her sister and grandma embrace each other under the rain then let go of each other to start dancing. Marisol spun around and sang words she was learning to use in Farsi. They were curse words and savory words. She was so proud to start taking on a third language. Abuela did the robot and howled out a laugh. Araceli and Marisol followed her moves then let loose with the cackling that was sitting in their guts. When Araceli thinks back to this memory, the three of them are frozen in time with their arms and chests pointing toward the sky. Their tongues are out for the sake of hydration. The rain continues to fall until the town floods. The three of them stuck in time underwater only to emerge to the surface with gills on the sides of their necks.

The Year of Tenacious Hair

Abuelita's hair wasn't a big deal until the year it grew at such a high velocity, she had to shave her head each morning to maintain some form of order on her scalp. Her hair used to be the color of clay in the depths of the earth, cooling browns, browns like dirt stained with fresh rain.

One morning, her hair creeped under the gap of her shut bedroom door. Her Chihuahua, Pompom, snuggled inside. A few cucarachas sought shelter inside sleeping Abuelita's hair. She woke up screaming out "mis amores, ayudenme" because her head hurt so much. Some of her hair was tangled around the nails in the walls and photos of me and Araceli. Her hair wrapped itself around her arms and legs. When we woke up she told us in a serene voice to find anything sharp and cut her out of her hair. Abuelita was always a morning person. Always. Araceli, Abuela, Mami and I found scissors and started battling her tangled hair. Cucarachas scattered and Pompom growled, but we were able to untangle Abuelita from her hair. The closer we got to Abuelita, the lighter her hair became. The roots of her head were all white and all four of us gasped.

The next morning, her hair wrapped itself under the bed and wiggled into the cracks in the walls. The following months, we took shifts to help her sleep in peace. We stocked up on scissors and asked neighbors to help us with her hair on Sunday mornings so we could take short naps. As the sun fell, Araceli stayed up past midnight and I stayed up until 3 a.m. Mami took the rest of the shift until 8 in the morning. I was delighted to see Abuelita's hair sprout out of her scalp and curl toward the sky. I braided her hair and stuffed as much of it as I could into my pencil cases and old backpacks. I hid her hair under my bed. Having it underneath me felt like a safety barrier.

There was a thrill in keeping something hidden for myself, like she was shedding her legacy and giving it to me in clumps of magnificent shining white hair. White like the snow I saw one winter, sitting on rooftops like a light dust, swirling inside funnels, touching the earth and then dissipating back into the gray sky. I wanted to hold onto the snow forever, but it melted on my tongue and into my stringy hair. Abuelita's hair was a tangible gift better than snow, better than eating hail, better than having to ask god to keep her here on earth until I have a face filled with wrinkles so she can take care of me into my old age. I knew I would have to say goodbye to her eventually, but having her hair felt like she was saving me.

Something in the air

Rumors about Abuela filled the air after she died. I told the neighbors that Abuela Rubí was born on the tongue of a blue whale and she rose to the shore with translucent jellyfish under a full moon. One crisp morning as I picked myself up from kneeling in front of Abuela's grave, a woman in red asked me if I knew about my past lives. I said no. She asked me if I knew the truth about Abuela. I told her I wasn't sure. The woman gave me a corn husk stuffed with mint, rose petals, and tiny pink seashells. She smiled at me and told me a story I wasn't sure I wanted to believe. She told me Abuela used to sacrifice men in the name of protecting the town. Abuela painted red across her eyes, her breasts, and up and down her legs. She collected ghost peppers, fish bones, rotting fruit, and hair clogged in tub drains. She minced garlic and onions and gathered the salt left on top of the graves of the dead who never confessed to their atrocities while they were breathing. She scribbled the names of the people who were forbidden from entering the town onto pitch black paper. She poured vinegar into an open gold-lipped oyster shell and mixed her collected ingredients. She added rose thorns and bur from sticker grass. She stuffed the notes into the mixture and then poured the concoction into a corn husk. She buried the bulging creation in the cemetery we stood on.

Abuela could sniff out liars. She smelled the tops of our heads in moments of doubt and called us out on our fibs. She was sensitive to the violence of men. She recognized the look a man gave a woman when he believed he owned her. She knew the shakiness in a man's voice when he wished he could be louder, when he craved a quicker tongue. She muttered under her breath when doors slammed. This power structure was violent in the eyes of Abuela, and these men deserved to be in the ground.

During the ritual, Abuela made the men drink white vinegar. She made them shave off all of their hair. Their eyebrows, their chests, their toes. She dug into the men with a small knife until she removed one part of their body. An eyeball. A thumb. An ear. She asked them to explain why they thought they deserved to live. She held the pieces of them in her soft hands and asked them to tell her a story. She stuffed the body parts inside curved seashells and asked the men if they could swim. *When was the first time you learned how to swim? When was the first time you realized you could drown a woman because of your own fragility?*

At the very beginning, Abuela selected men who were abusive to their partners. She could smell the fear on a woman or child, a specific sour sweat from the man, and she could smell salt and spit washed away and hidden from a woman's face.

After years of practice, she started kidnapping

local politicians who insisted we build more borders, more walls. Abuela lived in a border town her entire life. She witnessed deportations. She saw families torn apart. She understood the people who felt like shadows in moments of fear. She dehumanized the political leaders who dehumanized her neighbors. She placed a black pillowcase over their faces and dragged them to the Gulf of Mexico. She collected newspapers with their faces on the covers. She read quotes from their speeches aloud and then asked the politicians what they meant. *What do you mean when you call someone illegal? What do you mean when you call brown children a threat?*

Abuela had a super strength she claimed came from being born in the ocean. She picked each man up by the throat. She slammed them into the sand and told them to have an honest moment with their fear. She wrapped them in American flags and told them to ask their colonizing ancestors to save them. She told them to ask for the person they loved the most because that person would never appear before them again.

Borders

Araceli informs me we are in a border town and the other side of the fence is full of dangerous people. Drug people. Lost people. Coyote people. She overheard this information when the news was blaring out of the television in the pet hospital. Pets shouldn't have to be involved in the politics of people. Pompom isn't a revolutionary for any political movement, but I know he understands the purity of loving a grandma. *What would the news look like if dogs were in charge? It would be a god damn spectacular miracle.* I imagine Abuelita exclaiming this and slamming her fist on any flat surface in the Mango House. I ask Araceli if she has ever seen the fence lining the curving roads when

Mami drives us into the city. My little sister nods and I tell her, there are beautiful souls on the other side of the fence. Some of them are lost, sure, but the fire inside your blood which makes you love ferociously is inside the bodies of people over there too. There are babies and eloteros and mujeres who sell those amazing neon light-up toys on that side of the fence. There are abuelas and granddaughters and ladies who work in skyscrapers, with perfect hair and fancy nails on that side of the fence. There are forces of good and the essence of evil on all sides. Abuelita was born on that side of the fence. Our ancestors lived and thrived on that side of the fence. We are from here, but part of us is also on that side of an imaginary line.

Under the earth

TV is not bad for you in the afterlife. Abuelita told me. Find a shovel, go into the backyard, and bury it under the tierra so she can watch her god damn stories. Bury it with all the other parts of us we have placed under the ground. She knows about my poetry and Araceli's nails. She didn't think she would become so attached to a material possession, but here she is. She's in one of my dreams, asking me to bury her TV.

As she started getting older, memory began floating away. It started with Pompom. She kept calling him "Cuca." Cuca was the very first Chihuahua she ever loved back in the days when her hair sat in gigantic rich brown waves past her shoulders. She called me and even Araceli by random names or pointed at us and told us *ven aquí, vengan aquí mijas.* Then, memories she talked about over and over started slipping away from her. She couldn't remember that Mami's first word was "cosmos" and she forgot Abuela Rubí's birthday. She could not remember our tradition of going to the planetarium each year on the hottest day of the summer. She could never remember where she left her glasses or her favorite mug. She was our lost Abuelita. The memories weren't disappearing in any order. They appeared in a tunnel, white light edging out the corners of the memory, voices fading in and out, then poof, the memory was mist in the atmosphere.

Abuelita sought her dramas as a form of building memories. She called dramas her querido brain nourishment. The dramas told stories of people she didn't know or feel an affinity with, until she became so enamored, everything stopped and the house knew to become silent so she could watch her shows. We created a schedule around her favorite dramas to ensure no conflict. Eventually, we started watching the shows together. Dios mío, the drama was stacked and stuffed into every minute of those shows.

Abuelita told me she missed love triangles and silent tension. She missed the feeling of her heart palpitating and sweaty palms when she started falling for the unlikeable male lead. She knows he didn't deserve her, but somehow he is destined to end up with a woman who is far beyond his emotional depth. Abuelita was thankful the male leads were fictional. *Imaginate*, if one of them walked into her life as she sat on her floral couch in the living room, her clothes would be off in a second, no questions asked, no regrets in her soul.

Abuelita knows it doesn't make any sense she loves these dramas so much. As an earthling, she was so imposing and unafraid to challenge men when she had the energy. Of course, she misses the Mango House and café, but coffee with milk is nothing without her TV stories. She wants to feel the tingle of sweat on her mustache when her favorite character finally gets out of the grip of financial burden and stands on her own. She wants to scream when the male lead makes a mistake so obvious to the viewer, but why, why must he always have better luck than the female lead. She craves the guilty pleasure in loving these dramas. Abuelita demands we start writing these shows when we become adults. Give her variety and give her a man with more emotional intelligence for the love of all the forest and water gods. She tells me to bury her TV when Araceli and I finish writing our first drama.

Goblin

Abuela wore the mask of a goblin on nights she had trouble falling asleep. In her white nightgown and green goblin mask, she shuffled around the neighborhood. She ate pepino with limón and salt in a bowl and crunched with her steps. She picked up stray cats, gave them ancient names, and let them lick her hands with their ridged tongues. Black cats were her favorite. They visited her in the dream realm often. Their purring vibrated into her body and relaxed her into a profound sleep full of epiphanies and sea travel. She uprooted plants and stuffed them into her pockets after inhaling their essence and clutching them against her chest. She looked through exposed windows of her neighbors and listened for snoring, moaning, laughing, and thin silence only possible in deep sleep. She sat with her legs crossed on each porch of the neighborhood. The Mango House. The Lemon House. The Dragon Fruit House. La Casa Naranja.

With the goblin mask, passed down to her from Abuelita Araceli, she looked up at the dark purple sky and invited spirits to sit with her. She asked them to take a stroll with her. She asked them what food cravings sat on their tongues. She offered to cook for them. She built an altar for forgotten spirits in front of the cemetery. She hauled a stubby circular table to the end of the town. She covered the table with a red lace veil. She collected smooth gray stones and made a circle with them around the table. She lit one candle in the center of the table and left some fruit and rose quartz as an offering. She made a bouquet of desert plants with a white ribbon to tie it together and placed it gently on the table.

Only one spirit bothered to tell her what it wanted.

She wanted black coffee and homemade tortillas with frijoles and little cubes of queso melting within the rich brown mass. She was a spirit because she couldn't decide where she wanted to stay. She received offers to stay inside the ash of active volcanoes in Indonesia or trickle in between chunks of moss in the Pacific Northwest of the USA. She missed her family and wanted to stick to the desert dust of the border town. She wanted to watch her children grow up and sprinkle herself into their hair as they played in desert fields. She wanted to stick to their skin and wrap the particles she left behind as close to them as she could.

Exoskeleton

Marisol was sensitive to the moods of other people. Sometimes, she could see a ring of color around the faces of people she interacted with. Magentas and thin ribbons of indigo meant unwavering happiness. This usually vibrated out of the bodies of teens with new crushes and babies being nourished. Sometimes, she saw color vibrate around her little sister.

She saw foggy dark gray around the faces of two people. She knew it meant to stay away. There was a man who spoke with her in a dream. There were gray streaks floating around the crown of his head. His tongue was stained with ink. He told her he was going to remove every bone from her body to build an altar for the ghost of the man she will kill in one of her lifetimes. Maybe not this dimension, but it's bound to happen in another. He told her to find relief in this fact. Marisol could feel the bones in her hands separating and then reconnecting. Her wisdom teeth catapulted out of her mouth. The man picked them off the ground and washed them with his spit. Her ribcage cracked open and broke through her skin. The man tugged at her ribs and washed the blood off in rain water. Marisol watched as he tied electrical wiring around pieces of her with ivy. He smudged across her forehead with black ink and told her to wake up.

Marisol told Abuelita about this conversation with the gray man, and the hair on Abuelita's arms stood up. She shook her body out and told Marisol they were going to take a trip to the ocean. A family road trip with snacks and fighting over what radio station to play in the background as the sky became bigger. The family packed themselves into the van and Mami drove them to the ocean. They let the gusts of ocean air tangle their hair and embraced the bits of sand stuck in their teeth.

Abuelita wore white and asked Marisol to do the same. She constructed a crown with fern leaves and placed it over Marisol's head. They sat at the edge of the shore, hip to hip, Abuelita writing and reciting to the sky. She got on her knees and bowed toward the ocean, asking the ancestors to protect Marisol. If something happens to her, give her the means for survival. Give her the means to keep her hands clean of someone else's blood. Give her a thirst for solace. Allow her to work through bitterness by turning it into something beautiful. Protect her great- grand-children. If anyone with wicked intentions comes into town, make them disappear by any means necessary.

Abuelita kissed Marisol's beautiful brown hands and told her she won't always be on this earth in the very body in front of her, but not to be afraid or ashamed to have to ask for her help in the afterlife. Marisol held onto her Abuelita's hand and they listened to the whispering voices swirling out of the ocean.

The things we leave behind

Being in the desert during the summertime transports you onto another planet. Gravity pulls at your limbs, reminding you if you perish into the earth it's much cooler under the ground. Your body is wrapped and embraced in hot air. It feels like an oven is opening in front of your body, and the heat encompasses every inch of you. Invisible swarms of waves sit above the gravel of straight roads lining themselves in between brown cracked formations of earth. The desert sits still with spiny shrubs and unimaginable blue skies. Abuela volunteered at the border with a team of ten people. They hauled gallons of water for the folks who were crossing into the US. Abuela prayed for their protection and she prayed for bigger clouds. She asked god to envelop the sky with white clouds. She asked god to lead the lost travelers in the right direction.

Sometimes, the volunteer group stumbled across material possessions of the souls who couldn't make it. Rosaries. Tooth brushes. Bandanas. Slips of papers with addresses scribbled on them. Family photographs. Remnants of the people they may never see again. Abuela picked up the photographs and rosaries to make altars as soon as she got back into town. She mourned them. She couldn't help herself. These pieces of the perished brought her to her knees every single time.

Abuela was naturalized in her twenties. She learned every presidential name, she could list off each war America was involved in, she could tell you every single capital and recognized each state on the map by shape, she knew what oceans cradled the west coast and the east coast. She knew not to live in Oklahoma because of tornadoes. She knew not to live in Arizona because they were adamant on questioning and deporting anyone who looks like her. She held her hand to her heart, staring into a flailing flag she didn't believe in. She knew she had to assimilate in order to pass as a citizen. She was to become invisible. A person launched into soup or salad or whatever Americans used to describe the diversity they claim to be so proud of.

Abuela thought about the cousins she used to know and the pecan tree in the middle of her old neighborhood. When Abuela Rubí was a kid, Abuelita took her back and forth between Juárez and Texas. They lived in small spaces on both sides of the border. It all depended on what Abuelita could afford. Home was a concept for the future. When Abuela was a girl, she dreamt about being split in half, one side of her in the ocean, the other on land, broken tree branches piercing through her, blood flowing into the ocean and into the sand.

Abuela carried the heaviness of the heat and the sweat pouring out of her body as a reminder. We are delicate and brave in our composition, yet we teach our children to believe in political borders. We accept a societal structure that teaches our brown children to hate themselves. We accept borders as an excuse to dehumanize those who are not on the same side as us. Resistance is critical. It is a necessity. Abuela knew it was more than the beautiful brown skin she was blessed with. She knew patriotism was a disguised word for superiority. She knew there were people who hated every cell of her being because she was not a "real" American. She knew it was a horrific history and the romanticism of invasion and stealing from Indigenous people to gain power. America wasn't made for her brown body. She knew these things and understood the privilege of having papers. So, she kept praying. She kept praying for impossible requests.

The things left behind by the people who are escaping their mother countries are not to be taken lightly. No one says they want to uproot from their homes on a whim because the thought of America is so enchanting.

Guarded

Newborns smell like the inside of an exploding star. They smell like sprouting seedlings wiggling out of the ground for the first time. In the town of Nopales, we celebrate life and the perpetual human demise. When someone from Nopales gives birth, they stop by the Mango House because Abuelita is considered a guardian for new souls. She ties thick strips of her white hair around chunky ankles and miniature wrists. The strips are to stay on their tiny bodies for a full thirty days. Abuelita does not claim divinity. She merely sits with new parents and grandparents and listens to their worries. Her hair is a corporeal gift, so she gives it to them.

She listens to the women talk about their miraculous bodies. Some of them talk about being literally ripped in half. Placenta. Blood. Shit. Piss. Mucus. Tears. Some of them felt as though they were performing on a stage for the doctors and nurses like they were in the middle of a telenovela. Even with fluids glistening under halogen lighting, some of the women wanted to make sure the doctor remembered the new mother who shouted every single name in her lineage. Others talk to Abuelita about the bliss of hearing small lungs give way for oxygen and a beautiful wailing. Others claimed to see a glimpse into the future, seeing their child go from fetal floating specimen into a full-grown adult. Some of them have cried to Abuelita because they don't know if they can do it. She assures them, they can. They can bring a good human into being. Their muscles will fill with lactic acid, it will hurt, but they will still find ways to burst with love for this new precious creature. There will be genuine pain. This is an inevitable truth. Being alive hands us cruelty at any given moment, but we tend to prevail. We are formations of skin and cells and somehow we survive.

Abuelita started the ritual of wrapping her hair around the babies as a symbolic gesture. One that says you have been listened to. There is some-one here for you. This was true. She was open to phone calls and visits from anxious young mothers, or tired mothers, or depressed mothers. She was open to tell them, they are resilient bundles of cells.

PART 2

Angels

Mami used to tell us she knew who we were before we were even born. We weren't human—we were angels. She saw it in a dream. She selected us amongst the clouds, floating fetus angels attached by the heart, rooted into the clouds. She peeled soft petals from the crowns of our heads. She picked feathers from our backs. It's freezing in the clouds and her skin turned blue. Her hair froze in clumps and fell from her head. Warmth overtook her body when she saw us. She fell in love with my curls and deep brown eyes. She fell in love with Araceli's dimples piercing her cheeks like an invisible creature was poking into them. She fell in love with the scent of the tenderness radiating out of our tiny bodies. She knew we were going to swim from her body and change her life.

Mami told me she used to have a continuous stream of dreams about space travel when I floated in her womb. Her womb had stars swarming around inside like fireflies underwater. I imagined the fetus version of myself being delighted that these stars were compelled to guide me into warm water. Those were the moments I saw her on a pedestal, glowing and her skin shining. Those were the moments I wanted to cradle her in my arm. I wanted to tell her I knew there was softness behind her rib cage.

The thing about Mami was she shifted from a vulnerable feminine energy into a violent explosion of blame and shouting. She was veins and a piercing red face and we were in the way. I often thought she was stuck somewhere in her past and I could never reach out to her about it. Her past was none of my business. She took most of her history to the grave.

We shared moments of tenderness. I reacted with attentive eyes and a curious smile when she told me about her vivid dreams. I listened to her stories with sincerity in my bones. It was my genuine attempt to show her I wanted to love her as hard as I could. I was saving these vulnerable moments for memories. I could float through the synapses snapping and exploding in my brain to reach for these flashbacks.

In her dreams, there were often waves crashing, she couldn't swim and often collided with Orcas who lunged her out of the ocean water with their tails. She had another dream about looking into the eye of a volcano, her hand inches away from gleaming orange lava. One of us called to her, as she looked over her shoulder, volcanic fumes and ash filled the entire dream. In other dreams, there were times when a small child guided her into a sunlit room, reminding her she was once a tiny creature too. She saw herself as a child, playing inside a plastic blue pool. Miniature sharks swarmed around her and she couldn't help it, she grabbed one of them and bit at its head. Blood poured out of her small smile. Mami loved explaining her dreams because they weren't based in reality.

Mami slapped me across the face when I told her I didn't want any children. How could I say something so ridiculous? She dragged me by the hair when I told her I wanted to leave the Mango House. You don't know how good you have it. She screamed at me, told me I ruined the family. I ruined the family with my lies. Mentirosa. I only lied because the times I told the truth, I was treated with disdain. The man she was in love with was doing tremendous damage to my body, my soul, my core, my longing for survival. She married the Fake Father after Abuelita and Abuela left this earth. I asked her to listen to me. I cried and told her he was hurting me. I showed her my bruises. I pointed at the parts of my body he was touching while she was asleep. She asked him in front of me, if it was true, and when he shook his head "no," Mami looked at me with her red face. She told me to go to my room. I hid under the bed with what was left of Abuelita: her hair.

The times her hands flung at me, I stayed very still and said nothing. I knew how to infuriate her even more. I never cried in front of her when she slapped me. I only spoke softly when she was around. I tried to keep my speaking to a minimum. I wanted language annihilated from human development. I was an atomic silence. The house became a place of saying nothing that I meant. I was teaching myself to be soft. I was teaching myself to withdraw from her attempts at manipulation. I knew Mami wasn't always ugly, but I also knew, I didn't have to keep her close. I could let her go.

Mami painted our faces and told us we looked gorgeous. Araceli and I wore our calavera-painted faces with pride. I was fascinated with the afterlife because I knew Abuelita and Abuela were on the other side. I wanted to become a fading star in the darkest night of the year. I wanted to step outside of my body as a ghost and watch my corpse decompose, with my bones leftover for coyotes to discover. Mami told us Abuelita and Abuela were happy to see us thriving and growing. Mami told us she was very proud of our acceptance and resilience to change. I told her we had no choice. I lit a candle for Abuelita and Abuela and looked into the flames in silence.

The Holy Ghost

In church, I scratch at my head until it bleeds. The priest elongates his sentences. His voice crashes into the ceiling and into my throbbing head. Sunday mornings, I get up earlier than everyone in the house. I steal maxi-pads from Mami's bathroom. I line one of them on the bridge of my calcones. I tape the second maxi-pad on the outside of my underwear. I slide into white tights and add another layer with a pair of shorts. I duct tape the shorts to my belly and my legs and then put on my church dress with red roses clustered on the puffy arms and trim of the draping ensemble. This is my safety measure and my way to feel in control. This way god can't look up my dress, and anyone who tries to grope me will only feel smooth tape and chunks of cotton.

We go to church as a family. Brown bodies in floral costumes and clouds of perfume. I sit next to Araceli. When she knows I'm angry, she holds my hand. I rub my palms against each other and lick the residue of old dirt and forgotten handwashing. I pick my nose and leave the clusters of light greens and red speckles under the pew. I build empires of dandruff on top of the bible and I wonder if I could ever trick anyone into thinking my dandruff was cocaine. I have only seen cocaine on the kitchen table and pinky nail of my step-father. The Fake Father. He inhales fast, crouched over and crooked, his head moving in spasms. He shrieks when he finds his thoughts amusing. He creeps into the hallway and searches for me, I only know this because he calls out for me.

I envision him sticking onto the walls on all fours and crawling in circles on the ceiling. He digs under my covers as though he's burrowing into the ground and snoops under the bed reaching with the length of his arm underneath. He taps on the ground with his feet, faster and faster as he loses his patience. He calls my name. He rips all of the hanging clothes out of the closet and winks at me as I look up. He grabs my chin and tells me to get out. He grips onto me by the wrists and drags me into the living room. I try to crawl away, I scrape at the carpet, but he says he wants to feel closer to me. If I dance with him, if he can smell my sweat and the heat from my body, he can feel closer to god.

I don't know if I believe in god, but I believe in patterns and I believe in conjuring anything out of the core of the earth in order to get rid of him. He is not a father. I don't call him father. He's not like the boring man standing in front of this god-fearing audience. He is a man who survives in spite of his sins. He's not like any adult I have ever met because I only ever see my mami take care of him with rabid warmth like she's under a spell and a desperate clenching hope that he will change for her. I often see her pull at his unconscious body to make him comfortable in his drunken sleep. If Jesus died for me, then he died for this man too.

I'm convinced he's possessed by an evil spirit. When I envision him in memory, I can only think of him with peeling, oozing skin and yellow eyes. He scratches me and he probes and I am ordered to stay still. *Stay still. Stay Still. Stay still. Be quiet and don't close your eyes. Be quiet and don't hide from me.* When he enters my room at night I think of a Holy Ghost. White light beaming from outer space eviscerating anything I can see on the earth. I can look at the light but I can't see him. I can feel his hands imprinting themselves into my limbs and my belly and then I go numb. I ask for my Abuela. She comes into the room in her yellow nightgown. I can see through her and tears pour out of me. I wail and I wail and the Fake Father smacks me on the cheek. I cry in silence as the Fake Father launches his body over me.

Shrine

What does it mean when you call for help and no one shows up. It feels like drowning. Water rushes into your lungs and you grab at your throat desperate to breathe. It feels like molting. Your back hardens and your heart hardens and you think you can crawl out of your skin. There are parts of you to leave behind, but you can't let it go because he appears again and again. It feels like your ears popping so hard, a shrill elongated beeping haunts them until you can hear nothing. You sit in dark rooms and wait for someone to pour concrete or ice or the spit of those who never believed you until the room fills up and you can't scream. I used to have dreams about being attached to my mami's body by an umbilical cord. Belly to belly. Blue cloudy water all around us. Our bodies pushed and pulled and collided into each other. I held my arms around her. I squeezed her. I shook her by the shoulders and she was not responsive. I tried to scream under the water. Her eyes opened for a moment and I looked into them. Then she passed out again. She stopped breathing. Our umbilical connection was killing her and keeping me alive.

She drifted further and further into the cracks of the ocean floor. I struggled to pull her with me. I swam toward the light sparkling on the surface of the water. My limbs clumsy and heavy on their way up. The cord snapped and launched me out of the water. My body slammed into the sand. On the shore, I threw up salty black strings of hair and bile. I scratched at my tongue and pulled at the hair clogged in my throat. When I looked up, the full moon shrank, until I could hold it in my palms. I buried the moon under the leftover piece of the umbilical cord and palm leaves. When I woke up in the morning, the blood in between my legs dried into thick rust on the sheets and down my legs.

Washing myself the mornings after the Fake Father put his hands on me was the ritual that gifted me a small piece of sanity. In my black nightgown, I stepped into the cool morning and clawed at the ground. I was possessed by an extraterrestrial energy to scrape the earth. I shoved dirt into my armpits and between my toes. I spit long strings of saliva into my palms and smeared my face, then slammed my face into the soft pile of dirt. Before I got into the shower, I gathered all of my forest green A through Z encyclopedias, and I grabbed a hammer and a screwdriver. These were the moments I felt the bravest. I shoved all the books into the bathroom. I locked the bathroom door and piled the encyclopedias in front of the door. I placed the screwdriver and hammer in the shower with me and started washing myself.

In my best wet puppy impression, I shook my entire body out and drank the hot water streaming into my mouth. Crying became exhausting, so I opted for squishing my face as hard as I could to test out how much more I could take before I would combust. Blood and dirt smeared the white tile and swirled into the drain. Sometimes lizards watched me. Mami's screaming and slamming on the door did nothing for them. They only scattered when I asked them if I could become one of them so I could die faster, maybe smashed by a car, maybe eaten by a hawk, anything, anything to get out of my own body.

Only in soft noise

He used to joke about training you. Small puppy. Moldable specimen. A sponge, soaking in the oceans and rain drops and tremendous gray clouds. He snapped his fingers and you turned to face him. You looked him in the eyes. Blue swarming darts. He called your name and you whimpered. You could feel his hands pulling at your limbs. Your small body slamming onto the floor. Quiet darkness stuffed inside four walls.

Where do you travel to when your body goes numb. You enter portal after portal and find yourself in a domesticated environment. Portal. Four stale walls with peeling paint floating onto the ground and electricity pumping into the veins of halogen lighting. You are alone in this room. This is preferable. Portal. On top of a kitchen table covered in white lace, the blood in between your legs spreads. A chandelier of icicles drips into your hair and the goose bumps on your arms start to pop into ruptures of mist. Portal. Birds bounce off the walls but they never touch you. You grab at them and place the ones you catch into a pouch in your belly. Portal. The ocean in this room is on the ceiling. You reach for the water and a warmth rushes over you. You can feel your breathing normalize again, and when the room transitions into darkness, you open your eyes hoping to see the eye of a volcano.

You can count on the violent beating of your heart in your chest to bring you out of the portals. It bangs inside your rib cage and pulsates into your fingers. It beats against your head and you want to scream, but these are the moments you were trained to be silent. Subservient girl. Dainty synthetic breakable girl. Not real. Never real in the moments where he uses this power imbalance of man versus child. Power given to smarmy men who can keep secrets.

You don't know why. You went through a portal into the stale room with the dull lighting and peeling walls, and then everything came out of you. All of the blood rushing inside you poured out of your mouth, nose, ears, and from in between your legs. Blood filled the room and you drowned in yourself. It was comforting warmth. It relaxed your outstretched skin. You shut your eyes tight and saw light. Neon blushing pinks and electric blues. Resplendent existence inside your head. You opened your eyes and looked up at him. You screamed. Even when he slapped you, you screamed even louder. You screamed so the entire neighborhood could hear you. You screamed until the spirits in slumber jolted out of their beds underground. You shouted at him. *I will eat you alive. I will eat you alive. I will eat you alive. I will drain the blood out of you.* It felt compulsive and natural, but most of all it felt good.

The next time he snapped his fingers, you walked out of the house and ran to the cemetery. You sat with Abuelita and Abuela and told them. Even if they saw what was happening, you finally said it out loud. You asked them to lead him into the ocean. You told them reality was frightening and you felt lost. You showed them your hands. Trembling beautiful brown hands pressed against each other in prayer.

Cracks in the earth

Araceli saw her sister weeping into her palms, and she approached as soon as she noticed Marisol was out of breath. She didn't ask her what was wrong. She brought her peppermint tea and cleaned her face off with a wet rag. Marisol held her head down. Araceli told her if she wanted to shrink, she would go with her. They could fly on the backs of moths and feast on earthworms. They could live inside a maple tree and suckle on syrup until they died. Marisol remained quiet until she fell asleep. Araceli climbed out of their bedroom window and looked for her cookie bin under the ground in the backyard. When she found it, she poured her nails and skin into the hollowed out halves of an orange. She added sugar, caramel and white petals to the mixture. She wrote a message to her Abuelita and Abuela. She stuffed the note into the orange and then sealed the orange shut with honey. She wrapped the orange in white ribbon and held it up to cover the moon in her line of vision. She didn't want to disturb them. She wanted to ask for small favors. She wanted them to know Marisol's extraordinary soul was never going to dim. The women in the family were born stubborn and resilient. The Fake Father, the nameless man, tried as hard as he could to rip her apart. Marisol had no choice but to survive him. It wasn't fate. It was a mediocre man absolved of committing horrendous patterns. He made these choices by the weight of his hands and his body. He was treated like an exceptional being amongst a house of brilliant feminine spirits. He left his shadow behind and it was dragging Marisol toward cracks in the earth. All Araceli needed was a sign from Abuelita and Abuela. Send her a sign and she will know where to go from there.

A place with snow

Magdalena sends Marisol on a greyhound to Colorado. It is winter so she sends her bundled in a blanket, a turtle neck and two layers of pants. She tells Marisol her Tía will be waiting for her in Denver. She tells Marisol to collect snowflakes and to build forts made of ice. Marisol shuffles toward the back of the bus. She sits near the bathroom. The smell is sour and climbs into her throat every time someone wanders out of it. The bus smells like packing tape and the waft of snacks opened in the front of the bus. Marisol has no food or water with her, so she sucks on the salt of her arm. She thinks about getting lost at the first stop. She could become the adopted daughter of the gas station owner. She could organize the chips and candy and assorted nuts. She could sweep the floors and meet people from states she will never live in. She has a script ready for any police officer who questions her. She will claim amnesia. She will recall a shadow man coming after her. She will tell them, she's on the run. She is running away from the desert because the snow falls soft and delicate and it won't suffocate her.

Colorado

Tía Lucia greets you with all of her teeth shining, the moles on her face move with her mouth. She yells out "Hola, mija. Hola, vida." She runs at you with a blue and red jacket folded over her forearm. She fluffs the jacket out and wraps it around you. It's warm and makes woosh woosh sounds when you flail your arms around. The jacket says "Nuggets" on the back and all you can think about is chicken nuggets because hunger sits on your tongue. Tía lifts you up and kisses your forehead. Her aura is tender and you wish you knew how to show it back. She's family and you were always told: *you love your family no matter what.* You know you love her because she's the one who buys you books and sends you maps of other countries in the mail. You know you love her because when you think about her, your mind goes into a space of ease. Tía Lucia is brilliant and butch and you think she is so beautiful.

Tía Lucia explains she only has one bedroom in her apartment. The couch pulls out into a bed. She bought pink pillowcases and sheets to go along with a blanket sprinkled with red hearts. She tells you to make yourself at home. She has slippers waiting for you as soon as you get to the apartment, and she helps you change into rainbow pajamas. You want to cry because this moment in space and time feels unreal. You wipe your eyes and snot from your face and touch the turquoise walls of the apartment. You go into the bathroom and smell her shampoos and conditioners. You go through her clothes. You want to take one of her baggy t-shirts and save it in a time capsule. You want to take in these moments because, as you understand, this stay is only temporary.

On snowy days in Colorado, you count the snowflakes. White, beautiful, sparkling, floating giants falling down from the sky. You can see the intricacy of their geometric formations and they glow. The memory of the snow is so bright, it hurts your eyes when you think back to the first time you watched the snow fall in slow motion to the ground. Sometimes, the snowflakes are bigger than your hands. Sometimes, you catch the snowflakes and eat them, then spit out the melted snowflakes back into your palms. You take the pool of spit and snow and press your palm onto your forehead. You baptize yourself some mornings while you wait for the school bus.

Tía Lucia takes you to karaoke because she witnessed your living room performance extravaganza of punching the air and kicking to the beat of "Si Una Vez" by Selena. She asks you to pick any songs you want when you step inside the karaoke room. You choose songs by No Doubt and Alanis Morissette because something about the way they scream gives you chills and makes you feel bigger than you are. Blues and greens and reds pierce out of the lights above you.

You belt a song out and you scream until your throat hurts. Your tía applauds and you bow. You wish you could stay in that karaoke room forever because Tía Lucia looks like modern art with colors sprinkling themselves on her. She is a light. You want to be light and beam into the sky.

Karate in winter

It's dark. A street lamp glows orange onto the snow and onto you. You are alone in dark purple matching sweats. You dig into the snow and clasp your hands together after smacking the biggest piece of the body. This being's foundation. Your creation. You gather more snow, and even under the orange glow, your hands are bright pink. They hurt, but you're determined to make a masterpiece. He is made of three lumpy parts. Every attempt to smooth out his body makes him lumpier. You give him a baseball cap and tiny twigs for arms. He has no nose, but you poke your finger into the sides of his head to give him ears.

You name him Fernando, after your Tío who

plays guitar and encourages you to remain creative. *Write, mija. Draw, mija. Dance, mija.* You give Fernando a unibrow because you have a unibrow and there's solidarity in finding others who look similar to you. You tell Fernando about the atrocities of childhood like the real ones, the deep ones that will follow you into adulthood, and the ones where it feels like injustice but it's just your Tía not letting you track down the paletero for ice cream because it's winter. You whisper a secret into his ear and then take a chunk off of his face to eat some snow.

In Colorado, you have to learn proper English. Your English is broken and your home is broken, this sounds dramatic, but there's a reason why Mami is in Nopales and you are living with Tía. Tía Lucia, she embraces you and teaches you how to fight. "You have to learn how to defend yourself, mija." She places you into a karate class for a month before she has to take you back to Mami. Mami, who you say "I love you" to after every phone call. Even with bitter grit in your throat. You see her as more and more human with every phone call, less of a monster and less of a romanticized caretaker.

Fernando is faceless and your brain freezes. You find fresh fallen snow on your Tía's red Toyota and scrape it off. You explain to Fernando, sometimes life feels like your face is gone. You tell Fernando, sometimes life feels like there are rainbows in your guts. This is why candy was invented. You add snow onto his face and give him back his unibrow. You give him a smile and then draw one on his face. You ask Fernando about innocence. What does this word imply? Why are you innocent and why do you feel like a burden? What does your guilt mean? Why did the Fake Father imprint himself into your history? Why do you have to carry his face and his shadow in your nightmares?

You tell Fernando, life isn't fair and he will melt eventually and you will go back to the same city with someone who frightens you more than any story. You ask Fernando not to forget you or your stories.

You build mounds of white in front of the apartment complex. Short white hills sparkling underneath the moonlight. You kick the air and then kick one of the mounds. You punch another and jump on top of others to squish the snow beneath your feet. Tears line your face as you impale through the last mound of white with your feet. You tell Fernando you could easily destroy him, but you won't. This is how you're different. From the Fake Father and from Mami. You pat Fernando on the back and tell him you're going back to Nopales in the morning. You hug the lumpy snow and fall into the ground. You curl into the snow. Your head is spinning, but you go inside to the warmth of your Tía's apartment and kiss her forehead before you fall into sleep on the floor beside her.

A spiral

Marisol is matted sweat and salt. She peeks into her underwear to find the creature giving her nightmares about scorpions filling the sea. She pokes around the lips of her vulva and she curls her pointer finger in between the folds. Tucked inside, a fire ant stung her and then suffocated. Marisol scrapes the ant out and observes the balled up body in the center of her circular fingerprints. How did it decide this was the safe spot in her body. Marisol imagined neon acid pouring out of her crotch while she slept and a never-ending string of mucus attaching itself to the fabric in her sheets like silk from caterpillar spit. She woke up Araceli and asked her to help create a barrier. A safety barrier made of magic and maxi-pads. They snooped under the bathroom sink and took pads of all absorbencies. They went into the kitchen and took the sponges wrapped in plastic, promising no more residue, no more dirt. They took the tarot deck tucked behind boxes of cereal. Araceli took duct tape and helped Marisol stick the pads on, starting with her crotch. They stuck pads in a vertical pattern around her thighs and then added duct tape for good measure. They took packing tape and stuck the Magician card, the Death card and the Strength card onto Marisol's belly. The tape shrieked as Marisol spun around for it to wrap her. Marisol imagined herself as a tornado. She wanted to spin faster and faster until her feet launched her through the ceiling and into the sky. They took the sponges and taped them around the bottoms of Marisol's feet. Abuelita's hair was saved for Marisol's neck, wrists, and ankles. Marisol sat in tape and hair and laughed. Why did she feel so silly for trying to negate creatures who love to live under the earth? She asked her sister to run a bath for her. Marisol sat in the tub and asked Araceli to pray with her. What should they pray for? Araceli says they should pray for snow. Snow so high, you have to swim in it. Or pray for one of those slip n' slides to take to the cemetery. Maybe ghosts can join them. Ghosts like thick fog floating above the aisle of yellow plastic. Marisol's fingers pruned into canyons. She sucked the warm water out. Her ears filled with water and she could only hear her heart talking to her. Araceli brought a towel for her and helped her squeeze water out of the maxi-pads. They deconstructed the armor. Hair and dirt and pieces of skin latched onto the tape. Araceli told her sister they can show Abuelita and Abuela how they still do everything together, even when their hearts hurt.

Birth order

We call it the Mango House because it's orange-red on the outside and the living room and kitchen walls are bright dandelion yellow on the inside. Inside the Mango House, I fight with Araceli about the politics of birth order. I am older so I can stay out when the stars sparkle and I can play in thunderstorms. She's the little one so I protect her at all costs. I warn her about the dangers of rebelling against the rules of birth order. I tell her to pray for another sister.

According to the rules of birth order, I have to go outside with her so she's never alone. There's one morning where she wants to play with the water hose. She asks me to build an aquatic obstacle course, so I fill our plastic mini pool up. I place a jump rope in front of the pool. She has to jump seven times because she's lived for that long. I bring out chalkboard and start a tic-tac-toe grid so we can battle before she starts her aquatic adventure. I draw an outline for hopscotch. She insists on being a princess so I make her a blue paper crown. I start the water hose and make pools of mud in the bare spots of our front yard. Araceli is so excited. She hops on one leg while imitating a mariachi cry. She splashes in the mud puddle and I follow her lead. I jump up and down, mud splashes my legs and my checkerboard black and white shorts. I sing the clips of songs we hear from infomercials selling number one hit CDs, and Araceli plays drums with her hands against her belly and legs.

I step onto dry land and my breathing constricts. There's tingling up my leg, like it has fallen asleep, but the stinging makes me want to throw up. Fire ants swarm up my left thigh. I stop singing and cry out for help. They crawl up my leg so fast, I imagine myself engulfed under thousands of them. I smack at them as fast as I can. I see my life flash in bits and pieces.

First, I remember being called dramatic in class because I could faint on command. It was someone in class with green eyes. She was rude. I don't know why a flash of her face appeared. I saw my tenth birthday party. The Fake Father played a song for me. Mami applauded and kissed him so hard when he was done singing they fell over and laughed as they bounced onto the ground. Then, I saw Araceli for the first time. I was only four, but I held her little body in my arms. She smelled so sweet. She was warmth incarnate. She was an aura of softness. I kissed her forehead and I asked her how she felt to be out in the world. She yawned and showed me her tender pink gums. She stretched out her hand and grabbed at my hair and then caressed my cheek. From that moment, I knew she could save me.

I try to smash the ants with my hands. Their crushed bodies release a poignant odor. Araceli stomps across the yard. She grabs the water hose and soaks my leg. She screams with me and checks to make sure the ants have been washed off my leg. I tell her about the flashbacks, how I thought I was going to die.

According to birth order, I should be stronger. I have been told over and over that I cry too much. I cry when babies are born and when ladybugs die and when I think about spiders crawling into my ears. I have a tender heart. This is what Abuela always told me.

Araceli asks me if I'm okay. She brushes my hair out of my face and tells me I can cry if I feel like it. She doesn't mind. She carries me on her small shoulders and I ask her not to tell anyone. She promises she won't as long as we can get paletas from the freezer and watch her favorite show about magical sea castles. Araceli tells me she's serious, she wants me to promise we will watch her favorite shows with no complaints from my end. I nod my head and her majesty leads me into the Mango House.

Conception of an altar

Marisol falls onto the bed and she's crying. A sensitive body curled tight. The loss of Abuela launched Marisol into deep explosions of grief. She builds mounds of color with multicolored beads, sequins, and glitter in every corner of the Mango House. She pours salt on the front porch so the neighbors know not to come in. She pours glitter into her bathwater with pink rose petals and she cries into the hot water. Steam rises off of her skin when she steps out and the glitter sticks to her scalp and inside her nostrils. At school, she cries in the back of the classroom and her teachers all call Mami in a panic. They don't know what to do with this chillona. No se calmá. I tell her to cry in private.

Cry at the graves of Abuela and Abuelita. Cry far away from the walls of a school that will only indoctrinate you with more lies about colonizers being kind and deserving our understanding. *Okay, I didn't tell her that at the time because I was only four, but if I could go back, I would tell her these things.* Marisol's body contorts before she goes to bed. She cries in silence, her body convulses in grief. She cries while she's dreaming. She's the Mango House's own llorona. The only moments of peace are when she's so exhausted, her head collapses into the pillow. She snores and it echoes off the lavender walls of our room.

Both of our grandmas are gone and I've been hiding my grief. I sprint to the end of the neighborhood and cry into the bark of tall lonely trees. I cry as controlled as I can into my hands until snot fills my palms. I share the snot with the desert. I scrape my hand against the ground and hope the clear slime evaporates into clouds or comes back in the next life as a snail.

We have an altar in the living room for Abuela and Abuelita. Their photographs are in black and white. The altar is draped with a rich yellow cloth. La Virgencita's image is stuck to the velas we light every night. Marisol and I let Mami make the altar by herself even with our teeth gripped to our tongues. Marisol sticks notes behind the photographs. She prays to the photos every night and she cries into her palms. I will never tell Mami because I know Marisol needs to tell them the things she scribbles frantically every single night. I know she needs to call out for them, asking for signs of where she can find them in the natural world.

I tell Marisol we should build our own altar. We can hide it from Mami and visit our Abuelas in private when she leaves the house on long days of work. It could be a really small altar under the roots of a pecan tree or an altar in front of nopales sprouting pink and yellow buds. We don't need to over think it. Marisol grabs a photo of Abuelita from the linen closet filled with stacked papers and photographs. She finds one of Abuela. Our history sits in that linen closet. Spells and letters and stories we started writing for our Abuelas. There are photographs of gray waters and cobalt blue lakes, rivers gushing curved paths, Marisol and I with ocean water up to our bellies. Marisol grabs some of Abuelita's hair, and she cuts out circular shapes from one of Abuela's yellow nightgowns. I grab sage and coyote teeth and fill up a backpack with white beads to bury. We make a map on notebook paper. Our trail is curved and sometimes we have to scurry to get to the other side of dirt roads, back and forth in a zigzag. We mark an X next to a tree near the cemetery or where we think the tree is. We promise, whenever we get to the X, that's where we build our altar.

Map of the wars
we never started

Marisol found it strange when siblings waged wars on each other with their entire bodies. Fists slamming into legs and bellies. Short legs swinging up with labored grunts following their spin back to the ground. Cries from a pit past the belly into the core of the soul, flowing with bright orange lava, crusting over into charcoal and then erupting back up as a scream. The wide open mouths of the angry siblings. The injustice in losing to someone you love. The battle of the stubborn to see who cries first.

Marisol appreciated how Araceli followed her around, taught her what enchantment lurked in nature, and most of all, her ability to remain quiet with their secrets. The secrets varied on a scale of outrageous to very real, too real to tell the adults. Marisol only liked girls, she knew this for sure. She was afraid of giant squids. Seeing them made her spasm into panic. Marisol told Araceli about the Fake Father. All the things he did to her body. Araceli cried hard when she found out, but she kept her promise not to say anything aloud. Marisol still believed in mermaids, didn't care who told her otherwise.

Araceli wanted to say the same thing to her older sister, about liking girls, but was afraid of perhaps being overzealous with the idea of falling in love. Araceli was in love with chameleons, fictitious wizards, mugs with three-dimensional heads of dogs protruding out, girls with the names Miriam, Xochitl, Medusa, even girls named Sandy. She was in love with boys named Leo, Armando, Jose, and Liam. She was often dizzy when lost in thought about the many gifts the earth provided her to love. Araceli went into shock when she thought about the skeleton inside of her body even though she understood the practical logistics of her inner structure. She despised onions. She didn't understand how people could eat food that made them cry.

Marisol adored the density of sweetness built into the DNA of her little sister. There was wisdom in her overwhelming capacity to fall in love with the natural world in an instant. She must have been a matriarchal leader in a past life. Marisol swears she is only alive because Araceli is beside her in this sisterly journey. Even when she hurts, and this happens often, she knows she can ask her little sister for a hug, or space, or to sneak out of the house to visit the cemetery so they can relax with the spirits who see everything but cannot say a word.

Brighter sides

The same week Marisol started her period, she contracted lice from her cousins Osvaldo and Flora, who were visiting on their way from Florida to California. Why this sprinkle of lice decided to stay in Texas, Marisol didn't know. Her cousins picked at the plump, armored pests and squished them in between their nails. They told her it wasn't a big deal, they could get rid of them if they wanted, but the lice kept them out of school. Marisol shrugged at them. She claimed there was a plague following her body, even so, things could be worse. Things could be worse, she penciled in her journals. She could be dead. She could be part of a white Jesus worshipping cult. She could have fallen into the deepest part of the ocean with no one to hear from her again. Araceli could have been born in another version of this life, but she was born in this timeline. Things could be worse.

Favors from the sky

Ghosts must have a sense of humor if part of their daily routine is haunting houses and empty roads. It could be funny to see those with beating hearts so scared to face the inevitable truth after us all. So, they stand in the middle of dark curved roads and remind us we are alive. We are alive and then we'll die. When ghosts invade dreams, they give us pieces of their past life. This is why sometimes we revisit the same school or building. It looks familiar because it is, to the ghost wandering in your head. Abuelita left behind her TV. It flickers on and off on its own. Static plays throughout the Mango House. Infomercials swear they can change your life in the middle of the night.

Abuelita's room became Marisol's room. Abuela's room became Araceli's. Both sisters bolted up and ran to the living room. The TV was on, something whispered on the other side. Black and white. An empty room with a single chair in the center. The back of someone's head looking out a window smearing with rain. A flock of crows filled the branches of an evergreen. An empty room with two chairs facing each other. An aging hand with nails curling. Fog swirling above tranquil water until small white frogs leapt out one by one onto the living room floor. They popped into white goop. Marisol stuck her finger into the remains and tasted it. She said it tasted like sugar. Araceli told her not to do that again. The TV turned off and they went back to bed.

At night, they waited until they could hear the static and launched out of their beds. What else did Abuelita have to say? It was creepy nonsense but it was from Abuelita nonetheless. White petals fell into an empty room. A shadow stood behind the falling petals. A black widow, elegant and plump, grew bigger than the room, and the walls crumbled. The black widow crawled toward the Mango House, but the screen stopped her from going any further. A waterfall flooded the cemetery and the bodies underneath floated to the surface. Skeletal frames looked like they could swim. The water parted as the sky sucked up the flood. The scene ended with someone putting a candle in front of Abuelita's grave.

Araceli and Marisol ran hand in hand to the cemetery. Legs burning and turning into flimsy, wobbling, earthly imperfections. Araceli fell on her knees three times. The desert scraped off layer after layer. Blood lined her shins. She kept running. Marisol landed on her side and on her right elbow. Blood twisted around her forearm and wrist, down to the cracks in her palms and valleys of her fingers. Her side hurt, but she kept running. Lungs ready to explode. Flammable hearts running as fast as they could. When they reached the cemetery, the ground was swelling mud, earthworms exposing their shining bodies in the moonlight. Araceli hunched over, held onto her thighs and wheezed in and out. Marisol found a crumpled piece of paper on Abuelita's grave. She opened it, read it, and fell into the mud. She clawed at her thighs and her belly. She rubbed her cheeks and her nose, she palmed at her head and then pulled at her hair. She kissed her muddy knees and let out a cry. Abuelita sent her a message. *This body is yours, it will always be yours.*

PART 3

Pink skies inside the folds of your brain

We are not defined by our traumas. You repeat this in increments of three and then four and then ten. You travel back into your old room and into the closet. You can feel his hands and it breaks you awake. You are cemented to your bed. Your body still. Your eyelids pulled up little by little until you can see your old room. Your ears ring in and out until sound leaves you behind. You swim in silence. It is the silence behind a redwood giant. It sits inside the eye of a cyclone. It waits and then you remember again. Then again. Then again. Then again. Linear time is a gift given to those with better luck. Memories smack you on the back of your head and you nearly faint. You become as small as an aphid. You shrink into a grain of sand. You remind yourself, this person is in the past, he can't show up at your front door, he cannot breathe your exhalations as he sprawls his body on top of you like an animal waiting for you to suffocate.

New moon

Marisol had crushes on female musicians. She saw them as wild women, women who howled and scraped at stages with glittering fingernails, women who glistened in sweat. Marisol could only imagine they smelled like depth in a dark green forest. These women were thunderous and brave. Bigger than life. Eruptions from the cracks in the earth, filled with fire.

Puberty made Marisol a shy and nervous creature. It also fueled her anger. Her heart shouted when there was too much happening in her head. Thoughts latched onto Marisol and then bounced off. A spiral of internal arguments flew into her lungs and then she spat it back out as she banged her chest with her fist.

Marisol wanted to dissolve into a grey cloud when her nerves screamed at her, asking her to pay attention and to feel everything. Sometimes she could feel everything. Marisol wanted to hide the parts of her body blooming with hair. She wanted to hide her face. Going outside felt as though a beam of light followed her around, too bright to be a halo, too dim to beam her up. There were days she could barely muster words to the adults in the neighborhood. Maybe a sentence or two to the Doñas who were always kind to her. She nodded at the other brujas in the neighborhood. She was not keen on eye contact with men because eyes were honest. She was afraid of seeing shadows behind the pupils. She was afraid of seeing the gray crown around the head of men she barely knew.

Marisol wrote poetry until her hand cramped and then crumpled the papers. She buried the poems in the backyard. She burned the ones she was self-conscious about. She kept the poems that sat in her guts. She wanted the poems in the yard to represent something bigger than her so she named them after plants. The holes in the backyard multiplied day by day depending on how creative Marisol felt. She blamed the stray gang of Chihuahuas. She wanted to be a part of their pack or at least give them little denim vests with patches of her favorite bands sewed on, but those tiny creatures were not to be tamed. Marisol stuck her head under the bathtub faucet and then shook her head in clockwise twirls. Mist danced in the rays of sunlight illuminating the bathroom. She grabbed translucent green hair gel and smoothed it into her hair. She slicked it back and smiled. She wanted to cut it all off again, shave her head. She wanted to stop carrying waves of brown past her shoulder blades because they were magnetic to the eyes of men. In her silence, her hands shook when she passed men in the city. There was a part of her that knew they weren't all predators, it can never be that way, but she didn't want to let her guard down. This was how she preferred to survive.

She wanted to be a rock star who stomped on the heads of perverts. She wanted to scream on a stage until her ears bled, until the veins in her throat burst. She wanted to feel safety in her own power. She put both of her middle fingers up at the mirror and stuck her tongue out. Thirteen was the year she started wearing black. She wanted to blend with the night sky and pitch black moments in dreams where she searched for her Tía Lucia and then they both ran toward dark waters hand in hand until they drowned in the warmth.

Packet of seeds

A packet of wildflower seeds looks up at me from the sidewalk. Dandelions erupt through the cracks, like they are protecting the packet sent to me by wildflower ghosts. I overheard one of the Doñas tell another Doña that the earth would consume us before we destroyed her completely. I wonder if dandelions are the first rebels in the cause. Are they reporting back into the earth? Testing me. Testing us. Observing who rips them out by their roots. I tear the packet by the corner and build a soft mound in my palm. I fill paper cups with dry desert dirt and place in the brown and flaky seeds. I add water and mix with my pointer finger. I imagine the wildflowers bursting from the cups and taking over civilization. What if the revolution starts in the Mango House? Will the children of these wildflowers treat me with uncertainty and wrap me inside them until I become human gruel? Would they let me live long enough to see myself turn into another body, a taller body with hips and hair bursting from under my arms and a bush over the mound I stare into with confusion and disdain? If I swallow these seeds, will they propel the wilderness I feel inside me, the one I try to quiet down, quiet down, even as my dreams scream at me.

Heartbeats

You examine the mangoes on sale in beautiful piles of red and orange. You feel the firmness of their skin and stare into the colors blending together. Mangoes remind you of the heart beating in your chest. If you stare at a mango long enough, you can see it pulsing in and out as though it is breathing in a new life. You grab into a mango with your nails. Mango juice drips into your palms. You swear you see a man who looks just like the Fake Father across the mound of fruit. You freeze at first and then your instinct is to run, run hard, run fast, run until your legs become useless, until you can launch into the clouds. The sky is turquoise. Your face is red and hot, like a self-induced fever pumping smoke out of your pores. Tears streak your face and you bump into a blur of blue hair and crimson lips. She helps you up and all you can think to do is offer her the mango in your hand as an apology. You peel the skin from the mango and you each take a bite. Nectar drips from the sides of your mouths and you can't help but look at her lips sucking in the juice from the mango. There's embarrassment rushing in and out of your lungs. Your tears are dry and you want to hug this person you just met. She accepted your offering and didn't ask any questions about the frantic sprinting across a parking lot and consequent collision with her. Her name is Valeria and she gives you her address in case you ever want to share more fruit with her under the sun. She makes you nervous and she makes you calm like maybe you've met in a past life or maybe she was one of the faces you forgot when you woke up from a long dream.

Something in the water

Marisol shaved off her hair and mixed it with Abuelita's white hair. She braided pieces together and wore them around her wrists until the night of the full moon. She waited until Araceli and Mami fell asleep before she ventured out. She collected confetti, flower petals, red cardinal feathers, cut up photographs of the La Virgencita. She poured honey and maple tree sap into a hollowed out coconut. She added the braided hair and let the viscosity soak in. She mixed fern leaves and her collected items together with her hands. She kept the coconut under her bed, wrapped in red ribbon. She thought of purity and white light and what it would mean to see her Abuelas again. She turned fifteen and she didn't want to make an ordeal. She wanted to be alone and reflect as the waves of the ocean whispered at her. She wanted the stiff silence of fear to appear and then dissipate like a ribbon of air. She wanted to become a woman. A woman with no past. A woman with freckles appearing one by one as she let go of the unsettling darkness sitting in her bones.

In a dream dimension where the sky is lavender and pink, she stood on white sand and let the clear blue water cover her entire body. Her body vibrated. The veins in her hands and her wrists appeared as turquoise blue and her pulse resounded. She could hear her pulse all around her as though it was what kept this dream dimension intact. Her cheeks swirled with pink warmth, and the white sun embraced her bald head. There was comfort in every step she took under the water. She laughed and laughed until her belly ached. She was celebrating year fifteen in warmth. Like a mermaid, she sprang out of the water and dove in, leaping in and out with ease. Her tongue and fingertips became shimmering silver. Her hair sprung out into small curls and became white like Abuelita's. She celebrated being alive and celebrated her rebellious existence. Her synapses sparking fireworks. Marisol woke up smiling. Abuelita and Abuela left that dream behind for her when she needed it the most.

Thirst

Doña Leticia from the Lemon House asked Marisol if she wanted to share a drink. Tequila and a split open pomegranate. Reason being, Doña Leticia was mourning. Her baby dog passed in the night. Peanut was a good dog. Valiant and aggressive, his bark gave him the persona of a creature much bigger. Maybe a bear, maybe a velociraptor. Doña Leticia and Peanut saved Marisol on multiple occasions. They slept on Doña Leticia's bed with doors locked and baseball bats beside them. Peanut on guard with his sensitive ears. They were ready to beat the Fake Father if he even dared step in front of the Lemon House. That was years ago. Marisol prays for Doña Leticia every night even as religion leaves her cells little by little. They pick at the pomegranate and Marisol takes a shot. This is her very first taste of alcohol. It burns but she keeps it in. She waits for a buzz to take over her body. Her cheeks on fire and her mouth grinning, she tells Doña Leticia about the first time she met Peanut. A little white fluffball of a Pomeranian mixed with a Chihuahua. Peanut escaped to the cemetery often. Maybe he was a sorcerer in a past life, Marisol doesn't know, but she was out there one night lighting candles for her Abuelas and Peanut was running laps up and down the aisles of graves. As Marisol looked up into darkness, Peanut launched himself on her. He licked her face and barked in demand of belly rubs. She rubbed his belly and scratched his chin. His itty bitty tail wagged fast. Marisol cried with Peanut in her lap. She confessed the severity of her fear to her Abuelas and she wanted to taste death. She was swallowed by darkness. She wanted to sleep inside a shallow grave. But, there was Peanut. A little bolt of light. She thought he was a guardian angel. He followed her to the Mango House and as soon as she was inside, she swears, he ran across to the Lemon House and curled into the first step of the front porch, watching her. Doña Leticia told Marisol she always thought of Peanut as a reincarnated being. There were times when he looked distraught, as though he was thinking of a past life. He looked as though he knew mortality was a part of his fate. They drank to Peanut and when the alcohol latched onto their souls, they shared an outpouring of tears. Marisol was so thankful to know Doña Leticia and Peanut and she was so thankful for the times they saved her life. She prayed for Peanut to come back as a newborn child who would be so loved and safe. A body that wouldn't need saving. A body born into luck and warmth. She prayed hard and rubbed her palms together until it burned so much she swears she saw a flame burst and then disappear into the skyline.

Made for TV

Over the phone, Araceli confessed a new secret to Marisol. She was now a Korean Drama convert. She was on a marathon. She hid in her new apartment during spring break and watched as many dramas as she could. She mastered the skill of reading subtitles fast so she could embrace the subtlety in the actors' eyes. These dramas made her gasp, clutch onto her chest, they made her sob. They made her happy. She loved ghost romances and time-traveling historical dramas the most. She was a tad obsessed. She exclaimed with her pointer finger toward the sky, *I get it now Abuelita, I get it.* Over the phone, she reminded Marisol of their promise to Abuelita. They had not buried the TV from the Mango House. Marisol kept the TV in her bedroom in case Abuelita ever needed to say anything else to her. The screen remained empty and round. Even when she plugged it in, the TV remained silent.

What kind of story would they write for Abuelita? A love story for sure. Maybe a story about water witches. Water witches in love? Time traveling water witches? Two water witches fall in love but must run from persecution through magic portals? This way we can make up planets and sneak in some sci-fi. I think Abuelita could learn to appreciate sci-fi.

Scene: Full moon. Velvet purple sky. Seagulls shouting at each other. A woman with bright white hair wakes up in the middle of the ocean. Waves pull her under as she takes her final breath. All of a sudden a swirling portal opens up and a hand reaches into the ocean water. The woman with bright white hair is pulled out of the water and lands onto the yellow bench of a bus stop. Her clothes are soaked, hair matted against her face. She coughs out ocean water and inhales desperate hunched-over breaths. A small hand brushes the hair out of her face and smiles at her. It's a child in an all-white school uniform. The child hands the woman a brochure. It has a note inside to take the next bus. When the bus arrives, her hair and clothes are dry. She steps onto the bus and there's another woman sitting in the very back of the bus. She waves to her and says *it's about time.*

Let's name the woman with white hair Rosario. Let's name the other woman Nayeli. Let's give them sweet moments in the very beginning of the drama. They hold hands on the bus. Because Rosario is from the past, death follows her in the form of grim reapers. Men and women in black suits follow her into the future. They watch and wait for her to fall asleep before they approach her.

Scene: The focus is on a small pink house behind chain-link fencing and rose bushes in full bloom sprouting out of the garden. Grim reapers approach the pink house. All the lights come on in the yellow house next door. La Virgen de Guadalupe lives next door to Rosario and Nayeli. She chases the grim reapers with a broom and the jewelry hanging from her neck sounds like wind chimes when she runs. One grim reaper manages to go unseen. She sneaks in through a back window and finds Rosario and Nayeli sleeping next to each other. The grim reaper grabs Nayeli instead of Rosario and the portal she makes takes them into a lavender field. Nayeli remains asleep and the grim reaper sneezes. When she sneezes, the earth trembles and Nayeli reaches for Rosario, but all she can get a grasp onto is a bunch of lavender. Nayeli bolts up and starts sprinting to see if she can find a road or sign to get a grasp of where she is. She looks down at her hand and has a flashback to holding Rosario's hand on the bus.

Araceli insists there needs to be a love triangle in there somewhere. Maybe the grim reaper starts to fall for Nayeli? There needs to be a defining childhood incident that gives Rosario moments of vulnerability. Maybe she can't swim. Maybe she doesn't feel like an adequate witch because she can't save Nayeli. Nayeli is the one who keeps saving her. Araceli jots down notes, and Marisol hasn't said anything for a while.

Are you there, sister?

Of course. I am always here to listen.

Blurred into time

As soon as midnight declared Marisol to be eighteen, she drove sixteen hours to California. She met an older red-bearded man online. She messaged him about the women he photographed. Marisol admired the variation of bodies and ages of the men and women posing naked. He took photographs of women in crooked poses. He took photographs of body parts imitating alien creatures. Double-jointed hands painted blue, pulling at black hair. Beautiful rolls of a belly with glitter in between the cracks. Black hair covering one eye and an entire eye exposed with a translucent murky film covering the pupil and a milky tear streaming down one cheek. Mouths open wide with white tongues slobbering over chins, the spit shining like a slimy waterfall onto the sternum of the person stretching into an arch. Marisol wanted to be naked in front of a stranger. Someone she would never talk to again. She wanted to be ugly on camera. She asked him to make her look like a skeleton. She wore skull makeup and smeared it all over the motel walls. She smeared her lips over her wrists and she shaved her head in front of this stranger. She poured honey on her head. She painted her toe nails red. She took her finger and fish-hooked her cheek open and let out a grunt. She sat hunched over so her belly stuck out. She pretended to be pregnant with a succulent rooting itself to her uterine lining. She didn't say much to the stranger, but he told her she smelled nice and he told her she was weird. Marisol held her breath as his camera flashed onto her brown body. She wondered if this is what white men dream about. Having a radiant brown teenage creature making a mess of the sheets in an isolated motel room. There was no tension in Marisol's bones. She wanted to prove to herself she could be more than the body she was given. Who cares if he sees her like this. She can wear layers of colors until all you can see is the top of her head and piece of shit men would still ask her for a moment of her time. She could wear almost nothing and it wouldn't matter. Marisol will continue to be hanging meat to those who will never see her as a person. So, she searches for ways to see herself as more than the body she has attempted to escape out of since childhood. She finds a sliver of it in this moment. She walks out of the motel room in red lips, a t-shirt exclaiming I LOVE LA, and drives toward the ocean.

Milagros

Marisol believes in small miracles. Rain sprinkling the tops of our heads. The way the wind sounds as it slithers between branches reaching toward the sky. The fact she can sleep now, in complete darkness with knives on her nightstand. The way crows scream in order to protect their young. The way blooming plants smell in the forest. These are the little miracles she can appreciate. She's been working on her anxiety. Breathing exercises and sometimes kicking through cardboard boxes and ripping paper into confetti. Keeping the pile of shredded pieces in her palms and throwing it into the air. Letting the paper sit in her hair, pretending they are dandruff creatures belonging to her. Creatures she birthed out of another panic attack. Time stands still. She falls back into the child body. Her back slams onto her old bed. This is what she means by a panic attack. They've gotten shorter and the span of time for them to come around has gotten longer. It used to be month after month. She found herself on the ground beating her chest with her fist until she stopped wailing. The past few years, it's been about every six months. The moment taps her on the shoulder. She looks behind her and his face is a blur. The memories become muddled. Marisol is proud of herself. She doesn't cry anymore. When she feels the lump in her throat, she shouts at the sky. She shouts with a raw throat to the sky that this was never her fault. This was never her fault. This body she encompasses deserves to reincarnate into something like a new constellation or a swirling galaxy. She deserved so much more. She deserved so much more, but she gets it, being born isn't exactly fair.

Fuego

Marisol stands in front of the mirror with nothing but a pair of thigh-high stockings on and smacks herself in the face. She sucks on her beautiful brown hand, finger by finger, until all five are in her mouth. Then she slaps herself again. She pulls her hair hard toward the ceiling of her studio apartment. She settles into the sensation. Wanting to scratch and wanting to pull it all out of her head from their roots. She pulls out ten strands and looks at each root with care. She whispers to each one. She throws them into the toilet and flushes. She slaps herself on the ass and watches the handprint become a fierce pink. Almost neon. Almost otherworldly. The handprint spreading and taking over the right cheek. Marisol watches blood rush to her face. She pinches her nose with all her strength. She holds onto her nose so hard, blood trickles out. Marisol watches the blood drip down to her mouth, the curve of her full lips, then off her chin and down the lines across her neck, onto her belly. She spreads the blood across her belly and smiles with all her teeth. The blood continues to trail down her body. She continues to draw with her blood. She waits for her blood clot to build up, and when she feels it start to trail down her throat, she coughs it out into her palms. Salt and metal and slime. She stuffs the chunk of mucus and blood into the dirt of a potted dead fern. She washes her body off with hot water and watches the rest of her body become pink. She imagines herself as a newborn. Pink fluidity and warmth in the lungs. She sits in the tub, holding her knees, watching the blood trail into the drain. Her own pink scalding skin and pain with nobody in the way. Nobody there to make her feel ashamed for wanting to feel pleasure.

The magician

Marisol speaks to Mami on the phone. She keeps it brief. She doesn't want to stir anything up. She doesn't want to feel guilty for leaving her mami behind. She left her mami in El Paso and has never gone back. She refuses to tell Mami where she lives. She refuses questions. She won't answer them. Even when Mami asks how she's doing. Marisol keeps it brief. Like a magic trick, she's taught herself to say "It's good to hear your voice" and then disappear for weeks on end until Mami hears the shrieking phone and rushes toward it answering every single time with "Mija, I am so sorry." And sometimes there's nothing but silence on the other end.

They are all dust

I had a violent outburst. I didn't mean to do it. I was dramatic. You know how men express anger on TV shows? How they shove breakable shit from flat surfaces to express their outrage? I did that. I tore down curtains. I threw my blankets on the ground and stomped on them. I bit at my pillows until cotton chunks burst out. I tore all of my clothes from their drawers and I smashed the clocks on the walls. I wore my favorite white dress with pockets. I drenched my lips in red and I put my hair into a high ponytail. It felt good to make a mess and then dress up.

I drove as fast as my anxiety let me and spun out into a ditch. I crawled out of the car and dust covered me. I snuck under a wooden fence and started tearing out the grass and filling my pockets. My hands were stained green, like Vulcan blood, and I kept crawling until I found goats gnawing at tall dry yellow grass. I wanted to take one. These creatures are stubby, comedic, and strange. So, I picked up a small goat and ran down an empty back road. The goat cried out and I kissed the top of her little head and I told her it would all be okay. We will all be dust anyway. The people I love, most of them are dust. Now, there's a goat in my apartment and I think she's used to it. She's nibbling at the plants and she licked my palms. Her name is Sirena, and I plan on taking her to the ocean sometime.

Time travel

Remember when we painted our bodies blue and acted like water? We figured it started with soaking our skin in the color we thought of as water. Blue. Blue lips and eyelids and fingertips. Our smiles were bright and crooked. With our chests out and proud, we exclaimed we were water time travelers. Water compounded into a squishy human body. Water wanting to know what it felt like to stomp on the ground and remain intact. We wanted to feel like aliens. How would aliens react if they found this earth with these stinky people and these funny people and these clumsy people? The first thing we did was hide. We hid under cars and in the shrubbery acting as a guard to front yards. We hid our blue selves until we found water. We found water in the form of a swimming pool. Chlorine and floating plastic donuts and little june bugs ready to test your patience with their sticky legs. We jumped into the pool and turned into blue blurs. We were becoming the swimming pool. We were water laughing and pretending to be silverfish. We were unafraid of the consequence of sneaking into someone else's backyard because what could they do? We were time travelers.

The Mango House

Araceli and Marisol decided to take a road trip to the Mango House. The Mango House sits in another dimension. A ghost dimension inside Marisol's head but she wants to go back. They wanted to see who lived there now. They planned a conversation with the new owner so they could get inside. What about the colors? What if the house is a different color? What fruit has the house become? Marisol hoped to run into the Doña who now kept the town safe. Who was the honor passed down to? Marisol and Araceli had not gone back to Nopales since Mami told them they were forbidden from stepping onto that property. She said there were too many demons, too many reminders of how things used to be.

Abuela and Abuelita were still buried there. Who was looking after their graves? Marisol was convinced she needed to go back. She wanted to wander the neighborhood and say hello to the babies and the stray dogs. She wanted to kiss the dirt holding her Abuelas under the earth. She wanted to feel the walls of the Mango House. She wanted to smell her childhood. It was a mixture of roses and incense and Suavitel.

When Araceli and Marisol get to Nopales, Doña Alma waves them down. She invites them into her house. She calls it the Lima House. It's bright green, like moss sticking to the walls, soaking in the sun. She makes them a warm plate of frijoles and rice with soft corn tortillas. Marisol and Araceli eat with smiles on their faces. Nopales is like a land of myth. A place burned into their memories and as they sit in front of the beautiful elderly Doña in her house filled with religious trinkets, it feels like home. Doña Alma details the expansion of the town. Past the cemetery, two new elementary schools and new high schools. Children running around, painting little murals all over the place. It's true, as Marisol and Araceli step outside, staircases to most of the houses are painted in vibrant stripes or polka dots. Doña Alma said she had no choice, she didn't want to deter the painter from her passion so she has swirls of colors up and down her front porch. Doña Alma walks Marisol and Araceli to the Mango House and the sisters notice the sidewalk painted like waves of water. Water painted all the way to the edges of the house. They let themselves in and peek through the windows. No one lives in the Mango House. Doña Alma explains the hauntings. Well, that's what people said. Shadows lurked in the corners of your eyes longer than they should have. Electricity danced and flickered on and off to the rhythm of songs. Ash peeled and fell from the ceiling during the winter. Someone knocked on the windows during full moons, and when you opened your eyes and looked out, there was nothing. Just you and the moonlight.

Marisol laughed at the stories. She wanted to miniaturize the house and hug it. She wanted to fold the walls in and stick the house in her pocket. She wanted to take it with her because as far as she was concerned, the house belonged to her and Araceli. The Mango House always belonged to women like them.

The front door was unlocked. As they stepped inside they could hear Abuela telling them to hurry, hurry, let's go back out, the thunderstorm tonight is going to flood the cemetery, they need to collect rainwater and see which offerings belong to who so they can put them back in the morning. Marisol could see Abuelita's hair spreading from underneath her old bedroom door. She wanted to see how far the hair would reach. Maybe the hair could embrace her in a cocoon. Maybe it was possible to hear Abuelita again. Marisol called out for her. "Abuelita?" Araceli called out for Abuela. "Abuela?"

Then together, they announced, "We'll be back soon."

Newborn

Marisol and Araceli destroyed their first room in the Mango House. They took acrylic paint and splattered colors onto every inch of the room. They threw glitter on the walls. They stuck hundreds of images of forest trees and ocean waves onto the wall. There were collages of crystals on the ground. Amethysts. Rose Quartz. Jade. Purples and turquoise and pink infested the walls and the floor. They tore out the ceiling so the sun could shine through. A makeshift greenhouse for their houseplants.

Marisol tore the door from the closet and painted a door on the back wall. In this new room, they raised snake plants, spider plants, a weeping fig tree, Chinese evergreen, English ivy, a jade plant, a Boston fern, and succulents lined the edges of the windows. Wall ivy vines burst out of the cracks in the ceiling and clung to the wall. The new room was a space for breathing and a space for newborn plants to peek out.

No one was to recognize the room. No one was to mention what used to happen in this room. It became a new room for other living beings to thrive. It became a place for birds to nest. It was the only space in the Mango House that belonged to everyone in the neighborhood.

Doñas brought their offerings of white feathers and silk. They came by to talk to the plantitas. They stopped by to meditate in the center of the room. Children wandered in and painted suns and planets and stick figures of wild animals. The room was a newborn and the neighborhood was determined to nurture it.

Head in the clouds

Marisol waved to Doña Leticia across the street and watered the garden in the front yard and then moved to the garden in the back. She saw fresh holes in the backyard and wondered who was writing new poetry. Sirena chased bumble bees and then ran toward Marisol for a pet on the head. Marisol shut her eyes and soaked in the sun. The first time she learned a spell, it was a simple one. Abuela told her thanking the sun and the sky was a love spell. It was a reminder of the small things we take for granted. Always look up and watch the clouds. Find the animals. Pretend you can use the clouds as mousse for your hair. Always feel the rain trickle down your skin. Think of the droplets as small spaceships landing and splashing into another dimension. Always feel fear when the sky is warning you of a bigger storm ahead. Fear is okay, because we know how to overcome it. Fear is a reminder of our vulnerable state. Always try as hard as you can to listen to the history of the wind whispering in the trees. Listen for the prayers.

Mythological bodies

Marisol and Araceli decided to move in together so they could finalize their television drama for Abuelita and because Marisol wanted more space for Sirena to thrive in. They repainted the walls of the Mango house bright pink, to match the plastic flamingoes staring at each other in the front yard. They smudged the house with white sage and lit candles for any spirits passing through. They emptied the storage bins filled with photographs of the ocean, lakes, puddles, and desert rain. There were also spells and poetry stored inside. Some of the pages were affirmations to remind themselves of how delicate we can be.

They wrote everything they could remember from childhood and filled their bins with history. When Marisol wrote about Abuelita and Abuela, it felt as though she were writing a fairytale. She could not believe they were in her life for such a brief moment and then taken away under mysterious circumstances. Maybe they preferred to be mythological bodies. Bodies that could transcend space and time and what it meant to be dead or alive. Maybe they preferred to watch over her and Araceli this way because it's how they were meant to exist. Or maybe we don't choose when we die, but we choose where our matter can float around and send reminders to the living.

Marisol bathed Sirena in warm water and took a quick shower. She told Araceli to wash up because they were going to the cemetery. Hand in hand, they walked to what used to be the end of town and knocked on the gate of the cemetery. Crows sat on the skyscraper tombs and rain sprinkled the graves. The air smelled like childhood. It smelled like the first night Abuelita was under the ground and Araceli placed her ear toward the earth asking her why she left. She wanted to hear an answer. She wanted to hear Abuelita one more time. The air smelled like the first time Marisol went to the cemetery without her Abuela, because Abuela was living there now. Marisol brought her yellow daisies and pan dulce with café. She sat with Abuela until the sun fell. She told her about her day at school and how she was starting to grow hair on her legs. She told Abuela about her dreams, the funny ones like forgetting her shoes to class and the ones with little gray birds flying out of her eyes.

The air smelled like their first day in Nopales. It wasn't a place to start over, it was a place to catch up. They wanted to reconnect with the women who sat in their heads like myths. They wanted to reconnect to the women who rooted them and instilled the imaginations that saved them. They both looked up at the clouds and then at each other.

Remember when you said we were born in the middle of the ocean?

Yeah, I remember being born there.

I think it proves what I've been saying all along.

What?

We are a family of water witches.

Rios de la Luz is a queer Xicana/Chapina sci-fi loving writer. She is the author of the short story collection, *The Pulse between Dimensions and the Desert* (Ladybox Books 2015). Her work has appeared in *Vol. 1 Brooklyn, The Fem Lit Magazine, Entropy, Luna Luna Magazine, Corporeal Clamor,* and *St. Sucia.* She lives in El Paso with the love of her life and the magical beast known as Sleaze.

Special thank you to JDO (I love you), Jessie Rocha, Dom Chatterjee, Lidia Yuknavitch, Domi Shoemaker, Natasha Kotey, Cynthia Trevino, Monique Quintana, Gabino Iglesias, Christopher Rose, Pamela Santos, Constance Ann Fitzgerald, Daniel Elder, Cassandra Alicia, Jose Quintero, Marilyse V. Figueroa, and to everyone who has given my words a chance. From the bottom of my heart, thank you.

For more information on Broken River Books,

please visit:

www.brokenriverbooks.com

Follow us on Twitter: @brbjdo

Follow us on Instagram: @brbjdo

Printed in the USA
CPSIA information can be obtained
at www.ICGtesting.com
LVHW041954120823
754876LV00007B/521